THE MARVELOUS CATCH OF OLD HANNIBAL

Story and Pictures by Berthe Amoss

Parents' Magazine Press · New York

For a Place and Its People –
Pass Christian, Mississippi

It was a lovely day down by the sea.
The sky was blue and the air
smelled of salt and fish.

Billy walked along collecting shells. He saw his friend, Old Hannibal, cleaning a small croaker— a very small croaker.

"Hello, Old Hannibal," said Billy, looking at the one little fish. "Not much luck this morning?"

"Well now, Billy boy, I wouldn't say that," said Old Hannibal, not looking up from his work. "In fact, I'd say it was a lucky day, a marvelous catch!"

"But it's only one little bitty fish, Old Hannibal!"

"Ah, that's all you see now, my boy. But if you saw
everything I caught this morning, sure you'd say,
'That's a grand catch, Old Hannibal, a marvelous
catch, the best I ever did see!'"

"I would? How many fish did you catch?"

"Well, it happened like this," said Old Hannibal,
satisfied at last that the fish was scaled. "Early
this morning, before the sun came up, I set out in
my skiff. The sea was still and smooth, and I rowed
far out from shore, well past Horn Island.

You can be sure I didn't come too close
to that eerie place, for they say
the ghost of Stumptooth, the pirate,
still searches there for his lost treasure.

I rowed till I could see land no longer, and
the sea was so deep, its color was a royal blue.

I threw my line in, and no sooner did it hit the
water than I pulled in this very fish you see here.

That was only the beginning.
I threw my net out the back of the boat
and hauled in a mighty load of mullet.

Then with my spinning reel, I caught
a swordfish big as you!

I caught mullet and gullet, scrod and cod,
snappers and flappers, trout and sprout, cats
and flats, stripers and snipers—

till my boat was so full, one more and to the
bottom of the sea I'd have sunk.

I headed for shore.
Now, what do you think happened?

A giant Galathesis Scolapacus—that's a fish so
wicked and mean, no man has dared to study his
ways—spotted his dinner. It was my boat full of
fish. He swam right up, his huge jaws gaping wide,

and swallowed fish, boat, oars, and me!

There I was inside that fish. And, Billy, I'm telling you,
that's the darkest, blackest place that ever was.

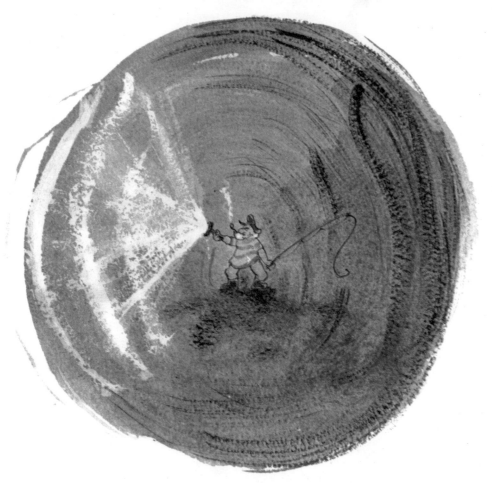

Lucky for me, I had my flashlight in my pocket.
I flicked it on and saw I was in the huge round
belly of the Galapacus Scalathesis. His ribs
gleamed white in the light. His gills blew cold
wet chills. It was hard standing up, so slippery
was the inside of that great monster of the deep!

I decided the quicker I got out, the better.
I thought fast. And then, with my fishing pole—
which, fortunately, I'd never let go—
I tickled that old man-eater's ribs.

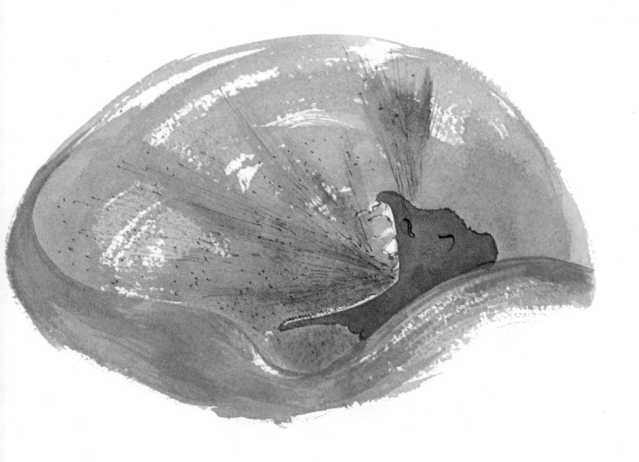

Well, he shook and rocked, he heaved and quaked,
he wheezed and then—he SNEEZED! He sneezed so loud,
it sounded like one hundred pounds of TNT.

And me, I started rushing through that fish,
upside down and twirling round . . .

till I blew clean through his nostrils!

That sneeze was so great, I flew along at
fifty miles an hour. I could see land,
and luckily I was headed in that direction.

Imagine my amazement when I saw traveling with me,
same direction, same speed, that very first croaker
I'd caught! I reached out and grabbed him under
the gills and strung him to a line on my belt.

By the time we landed, we were in shallow water,
just a few yards out from this very spot.

I waded in. And here I am!"

"But the boat, Old Hannibal, how did you get
your boat back?"

"Well now, Billy, I'm glad you asked me that.
As a matter of fact, I guess my boat gave the
old sea monster a stomach-ache and he spit it out.

As I was cleaning this croaker, just before you
came up, my boat drifted right in to shore on
the crest of the rising tide!

Now, Billy boy, how about this here fish? Is it,
or is it not a splendid catch, a marvelous catch,
the best you ever did see?''

"Old Hannibal," said Billy, "I think it's a whopper!"